The Magic Escapes

A Magical World Awaits You
Read

THE SECRETS OF DROON

The Magic Escapes

by Tony Abbott
Illustrated by Tim Jessell

A
LITTLE APPLE
PAPERBACK

SCHOLASTIC INC.
New York Toronto London Auckland Sydney
Mexico City New Delhi Hong Kong Buenos Aires

Book design by Dawn Adelman

ISBN 0-439-42077-6

12   7/0

Printed in the U.S.A.   40
First printing, September 2002

For Dolores,
Jane, and Lucy,
my life

Contents

Contents

One

The Time Before

"Race you to the top!" Eric Hinkle cried suddenly. He grabbed the branch of an apple tree in his backyard and pulled himself up.

His friends Neal Kroger and Julie Rubin laughed, then clambered up after him.

"I win!" said Eric when he reached the top.

A moment later, Julie and Neal were up next to him, clinging to the highest branches.

"I love climbing this tree," said Neal, twisting an apple from a branch and biting into it. "You get a reward for climbing it. And I have to say, Eric, your tree has the best apples in town. They remind me of your mom's awesome apple pie."

"That's Neal, all right," said Julie with a laugh. "Even food reminds him of food."

"Is there anything else?" Neal grinned, showing a bit of apple peel stuck between his teeth.

From the top branches, the kids looked out at their neighborhood. Their town sat in a valley nestled in the center of three lumpy hills, themselves all covered with blossoming fruit trees.

Two towns over was the bright blue ocean.

"It's almost . . . magical up here," said Eric as a warm breeze wafted into the tree-top. "You know what it makes me think of?"

"Yes," said Julie. "I'm thinking about it, too. And if Neal wasn't all about apples right now, he'd also be thinking about it."

Neal took a noisy bite. "As a matter of fact, I *am* thinking about it. Droon, right?"

"Droon," said Eric.

"Droon," said Julie.

Droon was the magical world they had discovered one day in Eric's basement.

It all began when they were playing around and found a small closet hidden under the basement steps. When the light was out and the door closed, the floor of that closet became the top step of a magical staircase.

Shimmering in every color of the rainbow, those stairs led down from Eric's house to a land of danger, mystery, and adventure.

Their first time in Droon, they met Keeah, a young princess who became one of their best friends. Together with the old wizard, Galen Longbeard, and Max, the spider troll, they were trying to keep Droon free from the evil clutches of the sorcerer Lord Sparr.

But on their last adventure, Sparr had uncovered a long-hidden *second* way between Droon and the Upper World.

The Dark Stair.

Long, long ago, a creepy beast named Ko had built the Dark Stair to enter our world. There, in the Upper World, he kidnapped the powerful and good Queen Zara.

That was terrible enough, but it got worse.

Zara's baby, kidnapped with her, grew up to become none other than Lord Sparr himself.

"I still can't believe Sparr is really from our world," said Neal, licking apple juice

from his fingers. "I mean, he's such a —
a —"

Neal stopped. He sniffed. He gasped.
"— pie!"

Julie laughed. "I've heard Sparr called
lots of names, but never — *pie*."

"No. I smell pie. Coming from the
house —"

Errrr. There was a squeak from the
back door. Mrs. Hinkle popped out and
called to the kids. "Time to come in. I just
made apple pie!"

"Woo-hoo!" Neal bellowed. "I knew it!
Have I got the nose, or have I got the
nose?! It's almost like I can predict the future!"

Neal jumped from the tree, bounced
across the yard, and dashed for the back
steps.

"Hey, it's *my* mom's pie," said Eric. "I

get the first piece!" Laughing, he raced Julie to the door.

But the instant Eric hit the steps, something happened.

Blam! Kkkkk! Boom! Fiery bolts of red lightning crashed and exploded around him.

"What —!" Eric staggered back.

The air wiggled and wobbled, a sharp pain struck him behind his eyes, and he found himself leaping, two steps at a time, up a black staircase.

"Oh, my gosh!" he cried. "The Dark Stair!"

With the force of thunder, it all came back to him.

Eric wasn't at home with his friends on a slow afternoon. He wasn't chatting about apples and pies. That was just a vision.

It wasn't real.

Eric was really in Droon, rushing up the

Dark Stair, trying to stop Lord Sparr from crashing into the Upper World. Into *his* world.

"Help!" Eric yelled. "Somebody help me!"

Far below, on the icy summit of Droon known as Silversnow, his friends Neal and Julie moved as if in a dream. Princess Keeah, her fingertips sparking with power, shouted, "We're caught in a spell!"

Even powerful old Galen, his long white beard flying as he turned, could not stop the sorcerer.

"Then I'm going alone!" Eric yelled. "Sparr's breaking into our world! I need to stop him!"

For as long as they'd known him, Sparr had vowed to rule not only Droon but the Upper World as well. And now he was almost there, racing up the stairs, his wicked powers blazing around him.

"My goal is so near!" Sparr crowed, leaping up to each step.

Eric hoped he *could* stop Sparr.

Ever since he'd been blasted by Keeah's magic, Eric himself had had powers. Some, at least.

And right now, he clutched the ancient Wand of Urik tightly in his hand. The wand had been lost in Droon for years until Eric found it. He tried to get rid of it, but the wand kept finding him, until Eric realized just how fabulous and powerful it was. It was a good thing, too, since now its awesome purple light cut a path through Sparr's red lightning.

Blam! Kkkkkk! Booom-boom!

"I win!" Sparr yelled when he reached the large, jeweled door at the top of the stair. The door swung open, flooding him with a strange golden light.

Laughing, Sparr leaped into the Upper World.

"No, no, no!" Eric gasped, staggering up the steps after Sparr. "What if the Dark Stair leads to my neighborhood? What if it goes right to my house — Mom! Dad! Watch out! Sparr's coming! He's evil —"

Bounding up the final three steps — one, two, three — Eric dived through the jeweled door.

What he saw shocked him.

"What? What?" he cried. "I mean — *what?*"

Eric found himself teetering at the edge of the top stair, looking down on a vast city.

But it wasn't his hometown. It wasn't like any place he had ever seen.

A crashing sea boomed all around the city.

"An island!" he gasped. "A *weird* island!"

Behind him was the dark outline of a rocky coast. Before him sat an island city of twisted buildings and flaring golden fires. Strange disks floated in the air above, casting light on the wet streets below.

And towering over the center of the island, surrounded by a maze of silvery canals, was a giant black fortress.

"This is crazy," Eric muttered. "This isn't my world. Where *am* I?"

Kkkk! The final crackle of Sparr's lightning faded, and the sorcerer leaped down the last few steps and into the tangle of watery streets below.

"Sparr! Stop!" cried Eric. But before he could follow, a sudden light caught him in its glare.

"There's one!" shrieked a voice. "And he has magic, too. A wand!"

"Uh-oh . . ." Eric spun around as three

bright patches of fabric — rugs — swept over the rooftops. "Magic carpets? In my world? This is nuts."

Sitting on each rug was a creature as thin and green as a string bean. They had long faces, pointy ears, and eyes that glowed yellow.

"Goblins, get him!" shrieked one of the creatures, circling its carpet. "He cannot hide!"

"I'm sure gonna try!" Eric yelled. Grasping the Wand of Urik tightly, he darted down the black steps and into the streets.

But the goblins were fast. They skidded their carpets to the ground and jumped off, their feet noisily slapping the damp cobblestones — *splot-splot*!

Eric zigzagged into a maze of narrow alleys. Running out the other side, he found the same three goblins waiting for him. "Fast, aren't you?"

"We have you now," said one, its green lips parting in a grin. "And such a powerful wand. It glows! Princess Salamandra will want it —"

Eric backed up. "Yeah, well, Princess Salawhatsis better get her own — this one's mine." He aimed the wand. It had only a handful of petals left, but its purple light was still strong.

"I don't want to mess with you," he said. "I just want to find Sparr and bring him back —"

Eric suddenly stopped speaking and looked down at the sparkling light. He knew the Wand of Urik possessed awesome power. Long ago, this wand created the rainbow stairs connecting Droon and his world.

But the first time Eric had used it, weird stuff began to happen.

First, Julie's cat, Pinky, began to bark.

Then, a bunch of hooded guys with tails appeared in front of her house, chanting strange words. Next, a huge ugly lizard soared overhead. Not to mention the pots and pans flying around his kitchen.

But the wand was the greatest power he had.

If he needed to use it . . . he would.

The goblins crept closer. "Salamandra must have the magic. Take it, goblins! Take it — now!"

Suddenly — *kla-bamm!* — a flash of red light blasted into the street from just behind Eric's ear.

"Aggk!" The trio of goblins reeled backward.

Even before Eric turned, a hand — with an iron grip — clasped him by the arm and dragged him into an alley no wider than a doorway.

Eric tried to scream but found he couldn't.

Silence! hissed a voice in his head. **Come with me, if you want to live!**

Eric knew the voice at once.

His heart leaped into his throat as he looked up into the burning red eyes of Lord Sparr.

* Two *

New Foes, New Friends

Sparr pulled Eric deep into the shadows. "Make no sound!" he said. He whirled his dark cloak around them both.

The goblins scrambled to their feet and peered into the alley, their yellow eyes blinking.

"Not here!" one said. "Let's try the next one!"

They splashed on down the street.

Sparr released Eric, but his eyes remained focused on the boy. "What is this place?" he asked. "What manner of trick is this? Where are we?"

"What? You're asking me? I don't know!" Eric said, his heart pounding like a hammer. "I mean, it's your Dark Stair. You should know —"

Sparr glanced up at the huge fortress. "Goblins? Flying carpets? Black towers? Princess Salamandra? Pah! This is not the Upper World! Where are we?"

"I don't know . . ." Eric stopped.

He was looking up at the fortress, but his eyes were drawn to what was behind it. Tiny, twinkling pinpoints of light. Stars. His gaze followed the shape of a cluster of flickering stars.

A handle. A cup at the end.

It was a shape he knew.

He gasped. "The Big Dipper!"

"What?"

"Those stars, I know them. We really are in the Upper World. But —"

"Shhh!"

More goblins were gathering, called there by the cries of the others. Now the street was crawling with them.

Sparr's red eyes flashed. "What I seek is not here. This is not the day I was hoping for . . . the hour . . . I expected something else. . . ."

"Yeah, well — me, too," said Eric. "I expected the mall or something. . . . Man! I can't believe I'm actually having a *conversation* with you!"

Sparr wrapped his cloak around himself, stepped to the corner, and peeked out. Eric wondered if he should use the wand on Sparr or escape. But in a flash, the sorcerer was back.

"We need to leave here. . . ."

"We?" said Eric. "No way. My friends

are right behind me. And we're going to bring you back to Droon. Keeah and Galen will —"

Sparr laughed coldly. "Galen is old, and this is not Keeah's world. They do not have the power we have. These goblins are after our magic. "

"Again with the *we*. I'm not like you —"

"Quiet!"

Another carpetful of goblins landed in the street. The green creatures shrieked loudly for others to join them.

"They will find us," said Sparr.

Eric blinked. "You're . . . afraid, aren't you? That's it. You're afraid. The big bad sorcerer —"

"You should be afraid, too," said Sparr. "You won't always have that wand to protect you."

"The alley!" shrieked a voice. "In the alley!"

The sound of slapping feet grew louder.

"Follow me!" said Sparr.

Eric didn't want to follow Sparr. Sparr was evil and cruel and wanted nothing more than to conquer Droon *and* the Upper World.

But his friends weren't around. The goblins didn't look like lifelong chums. And by the sound of it, there were more and more and more of them.

"Come!" said Sparr, holding his hand out.

"As if!" Eric snorted. He didn't take the sorcerer's hand, but he did follow him.

Splashing through ankle-deep puddles, the two flitted into the shadows. Only the red sparks from Sparr's fingertips lit the way.

The sorcerer dashed deeper into one twisting street after another. Finally, he stopped.

"They're still after us," said Eric, breath-less. "Why are you stopping? They'll catch us."

Scanning both ways, Sparr aimed his hand at the street, muttered a strange word, and — *kzzzt!* — a blast of red light shot from his fingertips. It struck the cob-blestones and blew a hole in the street.

The sound of water streaming below and a sudden strong smell told Eric what was beneath them.

"The sewers? Ha! You want to go into the sewers? I don't think so —"

"There they are!" a goblin shrieked. Now both ends of the street were blocked.

"Okay — into the sewers!" cried Eric.

Sparr slid down the shaft into a round tunnel. Eric jumped in after him. A stream of thick water flowed down the middle of the tunnel.

Eric pinched his nose. "Nice place you

found us. It's stinky down here. Very stinky."

"When you are hunted, you hide," said Sparr. He took off into the tunnel, the sparks from his fingers lighting the way. After several turns, he stopped, listened, then turned to Eric.

"Put out your hand."

"What?" said Eric.

"Do it."

Eric did what Sparr asked.

Looking both ways, Sparr pulled a small pouch from under his cloak, un-strung it, and shook it over his own palm. Two small shiny stones dropped out. Light streamed out of them, casting a silvery-blue glow on their faces.

The gems were carved in the shape of eyes.

"What are they?" Eric asked.

"The Eyes of the Coiled Viper," Sparr

said. "It is the Viper I seek in your world. But it is not here." He took one of the gems and held it up.

"There is power in this strange city," he said. "Power that may help me in my quest for the Viper. I must seek out this Sala-mandra."

He dropped the gem in Eric's palm.

Eric flinched. The stone felt like ice in his hand. Or like fire. He couldn't tell which.

"Why are you giving this to me?"

"For safekeeping," said Sparr.

"Safekeeping? But this is crazy! We're — we're — enemies!"

Sparr spat out a laugh. "We are much more than that, Eric Hinkle! You and I . . . our day is coming . . . the hour, when . . . but no, not yet."

Then, with his gaze still fixed on Eric, Sparr said slowly, "I can tell from the look in your eyes that you will not betray me. This will be . . . our little secret . . . our little secret. . . ."

Speaking that last word, Sparr stared deeply at Eric. It felt as if the sorcerer were drilling all the way to the center of his brain. His head ached, as it did when he had a vision.

Sparr put the other gem in the pouch and slipped it back under his cloak. "Be careful."

He stepped away into the shadows.

"*You're* telling *me* to be careful?" said Eric. "I'm usually being careful not to be *destroyed* by you!"

Whether Sparr heard him or not, Eric wasn't sure. For the sorcerer had already turned to the watery darkness and was running away through the tunnels. His footsteps echoed until Eric heard them no more.

"Now *that* was about as weird as it comes," he sighed. "Sparr telling *me* to be careful. And giving me stuff!"

Holding up the Wand of Urik to the small gem sitting in his palm, Eric saw something deep within the blue stone. Something moving.

Something, perhaps, alive.

"This is amazing," he said softly.

"I agree!" said a growly voice behind him.

"Uh-oh," Eric groaned. "Unless that's Neal pretending to be a goblin, I'm in trouble."

He turned to see a slimy green face peering down at him from a hole in the street above.

It wasn't Neal.

"I think I'm in trouble," said Eric.

"Goblins, I found him!" the creature shrieked, plopping down through the hole.

"Yep, I'm in trouble!"

Eric turned and ran as a dozen ugly goblins splashed after him through the stinky sewers.

The very stinky sewers.

Three

Adventure in the Night

"Get the human boy!"

His legs aching, his heart pounding, Eric raced through the tunnels, barely keeping ahead of the howling goblins.

He wasn't sure why or how, but a whisper in his head seemed to tell him the way.

Right. Now left. Straight. Left again. Left!

He wondered if it was Keeah's voice. Where, after all, *were* his friends? Hadn't they been just behind him, rushing up the Dark Stair?

"Faster!" cried the goblins, gaining ground.

Around the corner . . .

Eric slid through one more turn when he saw a shaft of light shining from the street above.

"Thank you, whoever you are! I'm free!"

Eric wriggled up and out of the sewers. The cool air of night was on him again. Overhead, the strange hovering disks glowed, and more carpets dipped and dived toward the big fortress.

Somewhere nearby, he heard the roaring of engines and the splashing of water.

"Boats," he said. "Probably going through those weird canals to that big black ugly fortress. It's like everyone's going there."

He shook his head. "Neal and Julie

should see this. They wouldn't believe it's our world —"

Sploing! A green shape sprang down from a nearby rooftop. Its large feet slapped the wet stones. "Give us the magic, boy!"

Eric shook himself from his thoughts. "As if anyone *ever* does what a slimy goblin asks him to. I think you'll have to — chase me!"

Eric ran from one black street to another, slipping finally into a narrow alley. He waited. A drop of sweat rolled down the side of his face. His pulse thundered in his ears. The goblin's heavy feet plodded by, then passed on.

Eric let out a breath. "That was close."

He looked around. He was right next to a courtyard of crooked buildings with steep, curving roofs.

And a pointy-eared goblin was perched on every one of them.

"Uh-oh," Eric groaned. "I think I just discovered the International House of Goblins!"

The creatures jumped down and surrounded him. "Give us the wand!" they cried.

"Never," Eric yelled. "It's . . . *mine*!"

The goblins howled and were all over him in a second. He tried to push them away, but in the struggle the wand was wrenched from his hand and skittered across the wet ground.

"Noooo!" he cried.

The goblins pounced on the glowing wand, shrieking, "We have it! We have it!"

Before Eric could make a move, the goblin thieves sprang into the shadows with the wand.

Others surrounded him. "Now, we get *you*!"

Suddenly, there was a great whooshing sound, and a strong hand flung down out of nowhere and grabbed Eric.

"Come with me!" said a voice.

Eric looked up. "Come with you — where?"

Fwoosh! Before he knew it, Eric was flying upward with a young man in a long blue cape and blue boots.

"Sorry to steal you away from your party," the man said, "but it didn't seem as if you were having fun!"

"I wasn't!" said Eric. "But who — whoa!"

They touched down on a balcony above the courtyard, then raced to the other end and leaped up.

"Yiiiiiikes!" Eric nearly choked as the two of them flew to the rooftop of the next building.

"You are awesome!" he said. "My friends should see this! If only I could find them —"

A rushing sound behind their heads cut him off. Two goblins on flying carpets dived in from different directions.

The stranger gave out a sudden, bright chuckle. "Goblins love speed. Which some-times works against them. Watch this!" He bounced across the rooftop, then stopped and twirled to the side.

"Akkkkgh!" the goblins howled.

The two carpets crashed into each other, and the goblins tumbled to the rooftops below.

"That is so cool!" said Eric.

"Glad you liked it. Now, let's move." Holding Eric by the arm, the young man raced to the edge of the roof and took flight once more.

Fwit-fwit-fwit! The cool night air

rushed over them as they leaped, light as air, from one rooftop to the next, goblin carpets diving in pursuit.

Eric felt like an acrobat winging from one building to another, stepping once, twice, then pushing off to the next rooftop.

"How are you doing this?" Eric asked.

The stranger grinned. "I imagine myself as a bird. It's quite simple, after all."

"But —"

The man took an impossible jump from the top of one roof to another far away, pulling Eric with him. Eric even thought he saw a flash of blue feathers on the stranger's shoulders.

"You've got to be a wizard," said Eric when they touched down.

"I am, and from a long line of them, too," the stranger said. "Come on."

Clasping Eric's hand, he sprang off the roof's edge and they glided down to the

street below, landing silently on the cobblestones.

"I've got to learn how to do this," said Eric.

The man glanced both ways, then grinned. "Maybe later, if there's time. For now, listen. You are in the goblin city of Pesh, a place that didn't even *exist* a year ago —"

Eric blinked. "But it looks so . . . old."

"It is old, but I can't explain it now. Beware of these goblins. But most of all, beware of their ruler, Princess Salamandra. She is extremely powerful. She collects magic. And people —"

"People? What do you mean —"

Whoosh! The carpet goblins circled the street.

"There they are!" they shouted. "Get them!"

The man turned one last time to Eric.

"Find your friends. Meet me at a place called the Dirty Plate — top floor — at midnight!"

Before Eric could say a word, the stranger did a double backward somersault — straight up in the air — and flitted away into the night, drawing the hordes of green goblins after him and leaving Eric stunned and alone under the stars he knew so well.

Almost alone.

"There he is —" shouted a voice behind him.

Eric groaned. "Not again!"

Four

The Princess and the Pie

Three cloaked creatures stepped toward him. Their faces were hidden under deep hoods.

"Oh, too scary to show your faces, are you?" said Eric, backing up. "Well, watch this!"

He leaped for a nearby rooftop like the stranger did but tripped and fell flat on the ground.

"Oww!" he groaned. He quickly flicked

his fingers at the creatures, but no sparks came out. "What? Oh, man. Anyway, don't you come near me!"

But they did. They surrounded him. Then, pulling back their hoods, they laughed.

Eric stared up at faces he knew.

"Julie? Keeah? Neal!"

"Helping you out — again!" Neal joked, pulling his friend to his feet.

"You guys," said Eric, catching his breath. "I thought I was all alone up here."

"You almost were," said Julie. "It took forever to climb the Dark Stair. We were moving in slow motion until Keeah broke Sparr's spell."

"And the minute we got here, you disappeared into the streets," said Keeah. "Galen and Max are somewhere, too, but the goblins chased us, and we got separated."

"We'll find them," said Julie. "Soon, I hope. This place is totally weirding me out."

Keeah handed Eric a cloak of his own. Her golden crown flashed in the light from the fires. "Eric, are you all right?"

He sighed. "Sort of, I guess. I mean, I'm as okay as you can be in the goblin capital of the universe. The problem is . . ." He looked at Neal and Julie. "Guys, I don't know how or why, but . . . this is our world. Look at the stars."

Julie and Neal looked at the sky over the fortress. Their mouths dropped open.

"You never told me your world has so much magic," said Keeah. "Or goblins."

"It doesn't," said Julie. "Where are we?"

Neal watched the flying carpets dip and dive overhead. "Some country they don't talk about on the news?"

"I don't know," said Eric. "But a princess

named Salamandra runs the place. It's called Pesh. Her goblins are stealing magic for her. They . . . they stole the Wand of Urik, too."

Keeah frowned. "We'll have to get it back."

"We will," he said. "Luckily, I met a guy who I think can help us. He is so cool. He even flies. But the weirdest part is that Sparr helped me, too. He actually saved me from getting caught."

Neal's mouth fell open again. "Whoa! Saved you? Are you guys best buds now?"

"Yeah, right!" Eric grinned, fingering the blue gem in his pocket. "But that's not all. Sparr also gave me . . . gave me . . . he . . ."

"What?" asked Keeah.

Eric trembled. His fingers touched the gem in his pocket but he could not grasp it or pull it out without pain shooting right through his hand. The blood coursing through his veins suddenly felt like ice. Chills ran up and down his back and neck. He felt dizzy.

"Sparr . . . gave me . . ."

Everyone was looking at him now.

"What did he give you?" asked Julie.

Eric finally wrenched his empty hand from his pocket. "He gave me . . . advice. He said . . . I should be careful. . . ."

Neal looked strangely at him, then laughed. "Sparr told you to be careful? So, the evilest sorcerer in two worlds is suddenly Mr. Nice-nice?"

Eric tried to smile. "Um, yeah, I guess. . . ."

Why can't I tell them? What's keeping me from telling them about Sparr's dumb gem?

Suddenly, that voice sounded in his head again — *Our little secret . . . secret . . .*

And Eric knew. Sparr had put a spell on him!

In the sewers, when he gave Eric the jewel, Sparr had stared deeply into his eyes. *It hurt,* Eric remembered. That was when Sparr must have done it.

That was when he cast some kind of spell over him. A spell of silence.

Oh, man, Eric thought. *This stinks!*

"What does Sparr want? Why did he come to the Upper World?" asked Keeah as more carpets flew to the fortress.

Eric knew what Sparr wanted. Something called the Coiled Viper. But he couldn't say the words. It even hurt to think them!

"Um, I don't know," he said finally. "But he wasn't expecting Pesh, that's for sure. He wanted the stairs to lead him somewhere else. It's messing up his plans. Plus, he was afraid."

"Sparr? Afraid?" Neal snorted. "Of what?"

"Of being captured by goblins," said Julie, tugging them all into the shadows. "Which is what will happen to us if we're not careful. Listen!"

Thrum-thrum! The sound of drumming filled the air. Then came the clashing and clanging of cymbals as goblins of all sorts — large, small, tall, short — marched slowly up the street.

"Our first goblin parade," whispered Neal, peeking over Julie's head.

"And I can just guess who it's for," said Eric.

In the middle of the crowd, four very large goblins trudged along, carrying a heavy golden chair studded with jewels.

Sitting on the throne was a young woman.

"Holy cow!" Neal whispered.

Keeah blinked. "Is that ... Salamandra?"

"Yuck," said Julie, making a face. "No wonder the goblins do what she says."

Salamandra looked human — more or less.

Her skin was a deep purple. Her eyes flashed with a yellow, catlike light. But most remarkable was the mass of thick black thorns that cascaded from her head and down her back.

"You call that hair?" whispered Neal. "You'd need a rake to comb through that tangle!"

Salamandra held a long staff. At the top was a cluster of pointed thorns that seemed to burn with a green flame.

The crowd passed slowly. Following Salamandra's throne were six goblins in black cloaks.

They were chanting strange words

over and over. "Om — yee — Pesh! Peshhhh!"

Julie grabbed Neal and Eric. "Oh, my gosh! Om — yee — Pesh? We've heard that before."

"You have?" asked Keeah.

Julie nodded. "When Eric first used the wand back home, and everything went nutty, these goblins suddenly appeared on our street!"

"I remember them," said Neal. "You mean *those* crazy dudes are *these* crazy dudes?"

"Om — yee — Pesh!" the creatures chanted.

Eric stared at the goblins. It was true. He remembered it all. "These are the same guys. And somehow they got from here to our home. Guys, I have a feeling we're in big trouble."

The procession drifted around the corner.

"We're in trouble, all right," said Keeah. "If these goblins appeared on your street, and Sparr is on the loose, and Urik's wand is gone — I'd say our troubles are just beginning."

"Thanks for making us feel better," said Eric.

Keeah smiled. "But we're together. And together, we can figure this out."

"I like the sound of that," said Julie.

"And I like the smell of that!" said Neal, pointing down the street. "Look!"

An enormous wooden cart, heaped high with pies, rolled out from the shadows at the end of the street.

Then they saw what was pushing it.

"Um . . . is that a . . . dragon?!" asked Julie.

"Well, a *small* dragon," said Keeah.

Behind the cart trudged a short, squat creature with brown spiky skin as rough and dusty as a potato. When he got half-way up the street, he stopped, looked both ways, then groaned.

"Oh, dear. Is Jabbo late? Oh, poor Jabbo!"

Tied around the dragon's waist was an apron. On top of his head, set between a pair of long, floppy ears, was a puffy, muffin-shaped hat.

"Jabbo is late, and Salamandra will send her green gobbies after him, dear, dear — oh — oh!"

The chubby dragon staggered back when he saw the children. His tail slapped the street excitedly. "Don't hurt Jabbo. Jabbo's only a humble little pie maker — wait. You're not gobbies."

"No," said Keeah as the four friends emerged from the shadows. "We're not goblins."

"And we won't hurt you," added Julie.

The dragon clacked his jaws, grinned, and bowed low. "Well, then. May Jabbo introduce himself? Jabbo is . . . Jabbo, pie maker to her royal thorniness. Would you like a pie?" He held up a large one, topped with a golden brown crust.

Neal jumped. "I thought you'd never ask!"

He took it and bit into it instantly. "Mmm . . . berry goob . . ."

There was a roar of engines in the distance.

"Salamandra's royal boat," said Jabbo, taking up the cart handles again. "If I am late to the fortress, I'll be late for the party. Big party in the morning. Can't be late for that. Can't be!"

"Wait a second —" said Keeah.

But the little dragon merely waved and

rushed his heavy cart away until he disappeared around a corner.

Neal licked his fingers. "Good pie. Very
good. I wish I'd taken two. Do you think
we should follow him? Aren't you guys
hungry?"

Julie rolled her eyes. "Neal, I think we
have to focus here."

"Julie's right," said Keeah, looking
around. "We came here to stop Sparr. That
has to be our main goal. Eric, did Sparr say
where he was going?"

Eric searched his memory. "Um . . ."

Don't tell them! It was Sparr's voice inside Eric's mind.

Eric clutched his forehead and silently
replied, *Get out of my head, Sparr!*

Sorry. It's all part of my plan —

Oh, yeah? Eric snapped. *Well, plan on
trouble, Sparr. Over and out!*

"Eric, are you all right?" asked Keeah.

He nodded. "When I saw him before, Sparr said he was going to find Salamandra. I think he's going to try to team up with Little Miss Tanglehair —"

You will pay for that, said Sparr.

Send me the bill! said Eric.

"If we're going to tackle Sparr *and* this nasty princess," said Julie, "then we'll need help. Eric, that stranger who helped you . . ."

"I don't know his name," said Eric. "But he'll be at a place called the Dirty Plate at midnight. On the top floor, he said."

Neal glanced at Julie and Keeah. "Didn't we pass a place with that name when we lost Galen and Max?"

"It wasn't the nicest place we've seen," said Julie. "Sort of nasty and creepy."

Eric grinned. "At least it's not in the sewers."

"Pretty close," said Keeah with a wink.

"Come on, then. It must be close to midnight. But let's be on our guard. We might see goblins."

"Or we might see Jabbo," said Neal, licking the last of the pie juice from his fingers. "If we do, I'm asking for that recipe!"

"Neal, focus?" said Julie.

"Oh, yeah, sorry. . . ."

Keeping to the shadows, and with their hoods pulled tight, the four friends wound through the twisting streets in search of the Dirty Plate.

Five

A Trick of Time

The Dirty Plate was a little inn leaning over one of the canals that led to Salamandra's island.

Even from the street, the four friends could hear loud talking and rough laughter coming from inside. Every now and then a glass broke. This was followed by yelling and thumping.

"I don't know about this," said Neal.

"Maybe we should wait till later? Like maybe . . . never?"

"It does sound a little rough," added Julie.

Keeah smiled. "To stop Sparr we'll need all the help we can get. Keep your hoods low. I'll take the lead. . . ."

Another glass broke inside the inn.

"That is, unless someone else wants to."

Neal gulped. "Not me. I'm just the funny one. You're the one with the powers. You go first."

"I agree," said Eric. "You're way more powerful than me."

"And way, *way* more than me," said Julie.

Keeah made a face. "Thanks a lot." She tugged her hood over her eyes, took a deep breath, and pushed on the door.

It squeaked open.

The room inside was long and low and filled with what looked like older goblins. Some of them were sprouting gray hair. Others had wrinkled green skin. They sat at small wooden tables, gorging on purple fruit pie and drinking cloudy liquid from glasses.

"This must be where the old folks hang," said Julie.

"And I see Jabbo's been here," said Neal. "Either that, or pies are the only food in Pesh."

When the four friends stepped in, the goblins stopped what they were doing.

Heads — sometimes two on a neck — turned.

One large, two-headed creature stood up. The left face was flat and green, the right one was pale and lumpy. It growled at the children, showing four rows of sharp teeth.

"Uh-oh," said Eric. "Trouble . . ."

Some of the other goblins stood up as well.

"I wish Galen were here," said Keeah. "Wait. I think he told me something once that might help." She whipped out a small notebook from her tunic pocket.

Neal blinked. "Crusty goblin types want to eat us and you want to drop everything and read?"

"Reading is educational," she said, flipping the pages. "You know I've been keeping a notebook of all my adventures. Here's the page I was looking for. I hope it works!"

As the goblins slouched over to them, Keeah murmured softly and sent a wreath of blue sparks around each of their heads and then across the whole room.

The goblins growled at them. "Grrrr —"

"You don't see us," Keeah said. "No one sees us. You all want to sit back down and eat."

The creatures stopped where they were. The one in front nodded both heads slowly. "We see no one. We think we'll sit down now. We'll eat some more pie."

As if in a trance, the goblins slumped back to their chairs and resumed eating their juicy pies.

"Keeah, that was very cool," said Julie.

"Thanks," she replied. "But we'd better hurry. Sooner or later, these spells wear off."

Tucking her notebook away, the princess led her friends across the crowded room and up a set of rickety stairs.

At the very top stood a lone door.

Taking a deep breath, Eric knocked. There was no answer.

He lifted the latch. And the door swung open quietly.

The room inside was small and tidy but empty. On a table near the bed, a thick candle flared, casting golden light over some curled papers. Julie went over to them.

"Your stranger guy left his light on," said Neal. "Do you think we should wait?"

"I think so," said Keeah. "At least until the spell fades and the goblins chase us out."

Eric went to the large round window and looked out over the crowded city. All across the sky, goblins on flying carpets were diving down to Salamandra's black fortress. Each goblin held a brown pack filled with stolen magic.

Eric guessed that the Wand of Urik was in one of those packs.

Down below, boats heaped with even more magical objects roared through the twisting canals and toward the docks under the fortress.

"What is this place, anyway?" Eric mumbled. "I mean, I never even heard of Pesh. This is our world —the stars tell us that — but there aren't goblins in our world. Where *are* we?"

"Um . . . maybe that's the wrong question, Eric," said Julie. "I mean, maybe it's not exactly *where* we are, but sort of, like . . . *when*. . . ."

Everyone turned to her.

She was staring at the papers on the table.

"This is a map," she said, running her fingers across one parchment. "A map of our world. Well . . . sort of."

"Sort of?" said Eric, leaning over her.

"I mean, we study these countries and oceans in social studies. Look, here's Italy." Julie pointed to a shape like a long, wrinkled boot.

"Here's Africa," Neal added. "I know that."

"But this is the weird part," said Julie, pointing to the corner of the map. "The date here says 1470. That's more than five hundred years ago."

Neal squinted down at the paper. "Why would the guy carry an old map around —"

"Because maybe it's not old?" said Julie. "I mean, what if this map has just been made? What if we, you know . . . went back in time?"

The gang stared at one another.

"Wait a sec," said Neal. "You mean into the past? Like some kind of time-warp thing?"

Keeah took a breath. "You said you never heard of Pesh, and goblins and magic don't exist in your world. Well, maybe they don't exist here *anymore*. But . . . maybe . . . they once did."

The princess flipped open her notebook again. "According to what Galen told us,

Ko built the Dark Stair more than five hundred years ago. Galen himself was just a boy. Well, what if the stair is stuck in that time? If it was, and we came up it, it would take us back to that time. The time when Ko first used it."

"I guess that would explain . . . *this*," said Eric. He ran his hand across the blue ocean to a green shape at the left edge of the map. "On this map, America hasn't been discovered yet. It's just a blob of land. No cities. No towns. No people. No *us*!"

The four friends stared at the map.

"Then we *have* gone back in time," said Keeah. "More than five hundred and thirty years."

"That would explain why Sparr didn't expect to come here," said Neal. "He came to the wrong time. He's stuck here. I mean now. I mean *then*. I mean whatever. Anyway, it's good —"

"Yeowwww!" A green lump suddenly shot through the window, struck the bed, and bounced under the table at their feet.

"A goblin!" cried Eric, jumping back.

"A *captured* goblin!" announced a voice at the window.

The stranger with the blue cape and boots grinned from the windowsill, then sprang to the floor, holding a big brown satchel. "I got me one!"

Six

Names to Conjure With

The goblin bolted up and pushed through the kids. "Salamandra will hear of this!" it howled. Then it leaped out the window and into the night.

"You get back here, Pointy Ears!" yelled Neal.

"Let it go," said the stranger. "I got what I wanted." He tossed the goblin's pack to the bed.

Eric gasped when he saw what was sticking out of it. "The wand! You found it!"

He reached for the golden wand, but — *fwoot!* — it shot across the room and into the stranger's hand.

"What?" said Eric, startled. "But —"

The stranger held up the wand. Its purple flower, nearly without petals, was folded to a point. "I lost it in a goblin battle yesterday and looked for it everywhere," he said. "I thought I'd lost it forever."

"*You* lost it?" said Keeah. "But Eric lost it."

The stranger's forehead wrinkled. "How could Eric lose what's mine?"

"But that's the Wand of Urik," said Julie.

"Sometimes I call it that, too," said the man, an amused look creeping across his face. "But mostly I just call it — *my* wand. After all, I made it."

For what seemed like forever, no one spoke. Eric's mind reeled with confusion until finally he understood. Then he blurted it out.

"Oh, my gosh — you're him! You're — Urik!"

The stranger bowed low. "At your service!"

Everyone stared at the man.

"Wait. You made this wand?" asked Neal.

"I did."

"This wand created the rainbow stairs to Droon!" said Julie.

Urik blinked. "The *what* to *where*?"

Keeah gasped. "Oh, my gosh. It really is true! It hasn't happened yet. We must have gone back in time to before the rainbow stairs were made."

Then the princess spoke silently to her friends.

Urik has never heard of Droon!

"I can hear you, you know!" said Urik, laughing. "In fact, I invented that little trick —"

"I thought Galen invented it," said Julie.

"Galen?" said Urik, suddenly serious. "Have you seen him? Is he all right?"

"Hold on," said Eric. "You know Galen Longbeard?"

Urik laughed again. "Galen *Longbeard*? But he's only twelve years old! Galen No-beard is more like it. And I ought to know him. After all, he's my pesky little brother! But what is this Droon place?"

Eric staggered back, staring at Urik.

"You and Galen are . . . *brothers*?" said Julie. "This is too much!"

The young man nodded. "Galen and I come from a family of wizards. For years, we have kept our origins secret, to protect each other. Our mother, you see, is the most powerful wizard in our world. Well, she was, until she was kidnapped —"

"Kidnapped?" said Keeah, glancing at Eric.

Urik glanced out the window. "I believe Salamandra had something to do with it."

"Uh-oh," said Neal. "Hold on to your chairs, folks. I feel another bombshell coming —"

"Your mother," said Eric. "Her name isn't by any chance . . ."

"Zara," said Urik. "They call her the Queen of Light."

"Oh, my gosh . . ." whispered Keeah.

At the mention of Zara's name, Eric felt a sharp pain in his chest. He had felt it before.

But there was something else.

"If Zara is your mother," said Eric,

"then . . . oh, man, how do I say this? . . . Then you and Galen — Galen! — have another brother, don't you?"

Urik nodded. "A baby. His name is Sparr."

The room went as quiet as a tomb.

Finally, Keeah spoke. "Eric, we have to tell him."

"Tell me what?" said Urik, his eyes darting from one to the other. "Do you know what happened to my mother and the baby?"

"You'd better sit down," said Julie.

As the candle flickered wildly on the table, Urik sat there, wide-eyed at first, then in tears as the kids told him what had happened.

They told him how Emperor Ko built the Dark Stair from Droon to the Upper World to kidnap Zara for her power. They told how she grew ill in Droon, while his

ZARA QUEEN OF LIGHT
& CHILDREN

baby brother, Sparr, came to learn the wicked ways of Ko. They told how Galen had become a great wizard, while Sparr turned to evil sorcery. And finally, how Sparr was up here now, seeking even more power.

When the children finished, Urik breathed in deeply. "I can't believe Sparr becomes what you say. I must believe there is hope for him. As his mother's child, there must be good in him somewhere."

"He wants to rule Droon," said Keeah. "If there is good in him, it's buried deep. And it all began when Ko stole him and your mother from here."

Urik rose and went to the window again. "It makes sense to me now. Three nights ago, we set up camp on the coast east of here. We came to try to battle Salamandra. That night, I was awakened by a cry. Galen and I rushed to my mother's tent. I saw a dreadful beast —"

"With a big hairy head full of horns?" said Neal. "And shaggy black fur and four nasty, creepy arms? That's Emperor Ko."

"Yes. He must have kidnapped my mother and Sparr, then put a spell on Galen and me," Urik said. "When we woke up hours later, we were sure Salamandra had ambushed us. We came to Pesh last night, but Galen was captured. I was trying to find him when I found you, Eric."

Eric nodded slowly. "I'm glad you did. But who exactly is Salamandra? Is she connected to Ko?"

"I don't know. She claims to be the Princess of Shadowthorn," said Urik. "If you can believe that."

"Why is that so hard to believe?" asked Keeah.

"Because the empire of Shadowthorn

vanished from the face of the earth thousands of years ago. Not a trace was left."

Urik turned from the window to the kids. "You see, our world is — was — a place of wondrous magic and joy. Then, one year ago — a year to this very day — Pesh appeared. Salamandra and her goblins began robbing our world, stealing magic to increase her own power."

Julie, Neal, and Eric glanced at one another.

"My mother feared no magic would survive. That's why we came here —"

Wump! Thud! There was a sudden scuffling noise outside the room.

In a flash, Urik blew out the candle. "Hush!"

Everyone froze. Keeah put her finger to her lips, stepped to the door, and yanked it open.

A bundle of furry legs and orange hair came tumbling in. "Oh, my! Oh, my!"

"Max?" cried Julie. "Max!"

It was Max, the spider troll, his eight legs all in a tangle. Laughing, Neal helped him up from the floor.

"Oh! My dears, I'm so glad to see you," Max said breathlessly.

The kids quickly introduced Max and Urik.

The spider troll extended a trembling foot to the wizard. "The brother of my master? Oh, but you are so young!"

"And Galen's even younger," said Urik. "If what your friends say is true, you've all come back in time. More than five hundred years!"

Max blinked. "Oh, dear. Then there are two Galens here. I lost the older one in the crooked streets outside."

"Urik thinks young Galen is trapped in that dark fortress," said Keeah. "So, of course, we're going there."

"There is another reason to go that way," said Max. "I have just spotted Lord Sparr crossing the water, heading to the fortress himself."

"I knew it," said Eric, gritting his teeth. "He's going to join forces with Salamandra."

Urik stuffed his map and wand into the goblin satchel. "If Sparr has even a tenth of my mother's powers, and he uses them for evil, then he and Salamandra together could quite simply take over our world."

"Both worlds," said Keeah. "That's why we need to stop them now."

"That pie maker guy, Jabbo, said Salamandra was having a big party in the morning," said Julie. "Let's go bust it up."

Urik laughed. "I can see you all like adventure. Well, I think we're heading for
one."

"Speaking of Jabbo," said Neal. "That
big purple pie I ate isn't sitting too well."

Urik stared at him. "Purple pie? You
don't mean to tell me . . . but only goblins
eat those!"

Neal's face fell. "Uh-oh. Now I did it."

"Typical Neal," said Julie, shaking her
head. "Only you would eat a goblin pie."

"As I recall, he wanted two," said
Keeah.

"But it was so tasty!" Neal protested.

A roar came from below, then a howl,
then heavy feet tramping up the stairs.

"Sounds like my spell has faded," said
Keeah. "We'd better get out of here."

Urik slung the satchel over his shoulder
and jumped to the window. "We could

steal some carpets, but I don't think we want to tangle with any more goblins. That means we go by boat."

Neal peered out the window at the choppy waves splashing in the canals. "By boat? With my stomach? Now I *really* don't feel good!"

As the small troop clambered out the window, Eric put his hand into his pocket. The gem was as cold as ice. He began to tremble once more.

We're coming for you, Sparr. . . .

A moment later, the six friends were scampering across the rooftops and down to the docks of Pesh.

Seven

Dangerous Waters

A thick mist was rising off the water when the small group approached the docks. The only boat there was an old narrow one. The paint on its sides was peeling and chipped.

"Looks like the goblins took all the good boats," said Keeah. "We could swim. . . ."

"Not in that water," said Julie, looking down. "It looks like fudge."

Neal groaned. "Please don't mention food."

Urik looked up and down the docks. "I wonder if my brother got this far before he was captured. He likes danger and loves boats."

"That's my master!" Max chirped. "Does he do disguises? My master loves disguises."

Urik chuckled. "Sounds like my brother. Twelve years old and always wearing beards and tall cone-shaped hats. Stay here, I'll find us a captain." He crept away quietly.

The old boat bobbed in the dark water.

"Keeah, can't you use your magic to get us a better boat than this thing?" asked Neal.

The princess looked around. "There may be goblins nearby who are collecting more magic. We'd better lie low."

"Good. Because my powers are acting weird," said Eric.

"Because you don't have the wand anymore?" asked Julie.

Eric wagged his head. "I guess."

But he knew what it really was. It was having Sparr's evil gem in his pocket that was messing up his powers. He hoped he'd get them back when he needed them.

"Humf!" said Max. "This boat is ancient. I wonder if it will make it to the end of the dock."

"I wonder if the captain will," said Julie.

Urik was walking back to the dock with an old man. A very old man. He was bent over like an aging tree. He wore a long, ragged coat and a floppy hat that sank down over his eyes.

While the man untied the boat, Urik took the children aside. "I know he's old, but he says he knows the way. It's too dangerous to go alone."

The kids looked across the water. The

canals snaked like a maze around the black fortress.

"Well, get in, if you're getting in!" the boatman boomed. "It'll be light soon."

One by one, they climbed into the boat. When they were all aboard, the old man dipped a long wooden pole into the water and pushed away from the dock.

Slooosh-ooosh! Soon, the boat was bobbing over the waves toward the entrance to the canals.

"Beware," said the boatman. "We are entering dangerous waters. These canals crisscross one another like a thicket of thorns. Salamandra has protected her fortress well."

"Thank you, sir, for helping us," said Keeah. "But why are you doing this?"

Without taking his eyes off the water, the boatman pushed his pole again. "Because you need help. Because our world needs help."

The small, slender boat glided into the canals. Ranged atop the walls on either side were cauldrons filled with burning coals. Golden flames cast wobbly splashes of light onto the waves.

The dark fortress loomed closer.

"I wonder what we'll find in there," said Julie. "Sparr and Salamandra swapping evil plans?"

Max snorted. "Him with his fish fins, her with her thorny hair?"

Eric wondered, too. What would those plans be? Could they really take over? Would Sparr find this Coiled Viper he was seeking? And what *was* it? Judging by its name, it didn't sound very good. Maybe if it were called the Fluffy Bunny instead. Eric wished he could ask Keeah or Max or even Urik about it. But thanks to Sparr's spell, he couldn't even form the words.

I'll get you for this, Sparr, he thought. *I'll —*

Leave me alone! Sparr's voice snapped suddenly. *I have my own problems.*

Ha! said Eric. *What kind of problems?*

This . . . Salamandra . . . she is . . .

What? said Eric. *Tell me —*

But the voice faded as quickly as it had come.

"Hey, Earth to Eric," said Julie. "You're mumbling to yourself. Is everything okay?"

Eric blinked. "Yeah. I mean, I think so."

There was a sudden splash ahead of the boat.

"What was that?" asked Neal, sliding over to Max.

"Ah, yes, I remember now," said the boatman. "These canals are the home of the kraken."

Keeah looked at her friends. "Please tell me krakens are nice creatures in your world —"

"Um, what exactly *is* a kraken?" asked Julie.

"Well, you might call it a sea monster," said the boatman.

"And what would *you* call it?" Urik asked.

"I'd call it a sea monster, too," the old man said. "But you can see for yourselves what a kraken is like. Here it comes!"

Roooaoooow! Two jaws full of giant teeth exploded up through the waves.

"Akkkk!" cried Eric. "It's going to eat us —"

The kraken's head was large and its skin rough and gnarly like bark.

Crunnnch! It took a bite from the boat's side, munched a bit, then came back for seconds.

"Down, boy!" the boatman roared, striking the kraken's knobby head with his pole.

But the kraken wouldn't stay down long. Its two enormous eyes glowed under the water as if they were on fire.

"It's coming back!" Max squealed.

The monster's spiky tail thumped the boat hard, throwing it against the canal wall.

The old man lost his balance and fell back.

Moving quickly, Urik saved him from toppling into the water. "Hold tight, everyone!"

"Not so easy!" yelped Julie, clinging to Neal on one side and Max on the other.

Urik whacked at the spiky beast with the captain's pole, but the kraken merely snapped off the end of the pole and swallowed it.

"I think Salamandra is trying to tell us something," said Neal. "Like — keep out!"

"I have an idea," said Keeah. She aimed her hands at a flaming cauldron on top of a nearby wall and sent a bolt of blue light at it.

Kkk-blam! The cauldron tumbled over, spilling its flaming coals into the water.

Ssss! The water hissed and bubbled for a moment before the coals were extinguished.

Kkk-blam! Keeah toppled another cauldron into the canal. Then another and another. Five, six, ten cauldrons of flaming coals spilled into the water, blasting the creature with jolts of heat.

"Take that, kraken!" said the princess.

Roooaooooow! The monster howled once, then dived beneath the bubbling surface.

The water went silent and still.

"Keeah," said Eric, "I think you did it."

"She did it, all right," said Urik, staring into the water. "She made it mad. Neal, watch out!"

The monster burst through the surface again, whipped its tail out, and knocked Neal over the side. *Splash!*

"Neal!" Eric shouted, clutching wildly at his friend's hands.

The kraken wrapped its tail around the boat and lifted it up into the air. *Roooaarrrr!*

When the creature let go, the boat thudded down to the water, and the children and Max were thrown out — *splash-splash-splash!*

The boatman and Urik still clung to the side, batting the kraken with the remains of the pole.

"Go to the fortress!" cried Urik. "Find my young brother, Galen. And stop Sparr!"

"We'll — blub! — try!" Eric shouted back.

Then the children and Max bobbed up one last time before they were swallowed by the deep, cold, fudge-thick black water.

Eight

Searching for Nobeard

Eric struggled to get to the surface, but the weight of his cloak dragged him down.

He flicked his fingers, but no sparks came.

Eric! Use your power! a voice whispered.

I can't — blub! blub! — my magic is —

The power is . . . in your pocket!

Eric clawed at the water. *Sparr? I'm not using your dumb evil powers!*

Eric groped upward until he thought his lungs would burst. Finally — *splash!* — he broke through the surface and drew in a huge breath.

"Eric!" cried Keeah, pulling herself up to the island, then crawling over to help him. "I was trying to talk to you, but you didn't answer."

Eric panted heavily as he took her hand. "Sorry," he mumbled. "I was on another line."

"What?"

"Nothing," he said. "I couldn't hear you. In fact, my powers haven't worked right ever since I saw Sparr."

Eric slipped his hand into his pants pocket. The gem was still there. Instantly, his head began to hurt again, and he grew hot, as if he might faint.

He knew his powers wouldn't work as long as Sparr's magic was in his pocket.

"Over here!" yelled Julie as a black wave pulled her away from the craggy shore.

Keeah and Eric ran to help her. Neal and Max bobbed up nearby and swam to Julie. Together, they pulled her up onto the island.

"Thanks," she said.

"Where's Urik and the old guy?" asked Neal.

"Still fighting the kraken," said Max, shaking the water from his spider fur.

The children looked back over the water. The boatman was struggling with the sea monster's tail, while Urik was using the wand to try to hypnotize it. But the kraken wouldn't slow down. Instead it dragged the little boat back into the canals.

"Urik told us what to do," said Julie.

"We need to find Galen's younger self before we can stop Sparr and Salamandra —"

Thomp . . . thomp . . . .

"Goblins!" said Keeah. "Hide!"

The kids scrambled to the shelter of a low rock as a troop of mean-faced goblins passed by. Each carried a bundle of stolen objects just like Urik's satchel.

"Thieves," Neal whispered. "Stealing magic from our world."

A minute later, the goblins were gone.

"They went in there," said Max, pointing to an outline on the rocks that looked like a door.

"And exactly how do we get in?" said Julie.

"Allow me," said Keeah. She turned to make sure there were no more goblins approaching. Then, murmuring a few words, she aimed her right hand. A single blue spark shot from the tip of her finger.

Pop! Errk! The door scraped open.

Lighting the way with a stream of blue light, Keeah led the group into a narrow cavelike passage under the fortress.

"All right, then," chirped Max. "Let's find my master, *before* he was my master!"

The passages zigzagged through the rock for a long while, then circled up in a long, coiling stairway.

"Oh, man," said Neal as they made the long trudge up the steps. "Getting a little dizzy here."

"Neal," said Julie, "you sort of always were."

"I guess that's sort of true," he said.

Max scampered along with Keeah. "To think that my young master is a prisoner in this awful place. And that Urik and — Sparr — are Galen's brothers, and all of them from this world! How is one to take all that?"

Keeah shook her head. "Old Galen has a lot of explaining to do. Talk about secrets. All this time, we've been battling his brother."

"He must feel terrible about it," said Julie.

Eric wondered if what Urik said was true. Was there hope for Sparr? Was there *good* in him?

"Wait —" Keeah stopped and leaned forward. "I see something. A light . . ."

"Is it the dungeon where my master is being held prisoner?" asked Max.

Thwack! Wump! "Arrrgh!"

A goblin came tumbling down the hall and rolled into a heap at their feet.

"A little boy!" it groaned. "And — oww! — so strong!"

"Um, *prisoner* may not be the right word," said Julie.

An instant later, a young boy in a bright green tunic and green boots tore down the passage toward them.

"Galen!" said Keeah.

He screeched to a halt and blinked at the kids. "Well, yes, but — excuse me!" He grabbed the goblin by its ears and pulled it up. "Try to put me in chains, will you? Talk! Or grunt or sing or do whatever goblins do, but tell me what's going on!"

The goblin wriggled to get free but couldn't. "The one named . . . Sparr . . . is in the throne room . . . with our princess!"

"Sparr?" snapped Galen. "That's nutty. He's just a baby —"

"What are they planning?" Keeah interrupted.

The goblin glared at her. "Something about . . . a Coiled Viper — arrrgh!" With one swift move, the goblin wiggled free of

Galen's grasp and shot down the passage into the darkness.

The young wizard looked at the children. "What is going *on* here?" he demanded. "Sparr is in this fortress? And what is this Coiled Viper? I've never heard of it!"

"I have," said Eric.

Say nothing! Sparr hissed in his head.

Eric ignored the words and the ache in his forehead. "The Coiled Viper is why Sparr came to our world," he said. "It's something with lots of power, and he's after it."

Galen put a hand on Eric's forehead. "Um . . . the last time I checked, Sparr wasn't playing with vipers of any kind. He's still a baby!"

The children looked at one another. They shrugged, they sighed, then they told Galen everything they had told his older brother, Urik.

How they had come up the Dark Stair, how long ago for them, but just recently for him, Ko had kidnapped his mother and brother. How over the years Ko taught Sparr to be a master of evil powers in Droon. And how they were following the grown-up Sparr now because they feared he would join with Salamandra to conquer both worlds.

Galen stared at them. Then — *wham!* — he angrily slammed his hand at the passage wall and broke a small hole in it with his fist. "I . . . I . . . What you say is unbelievable. Sparr on a quest for magic? This is not good —"

"But maybe it's not so bad," said Eric. "Whatever the Coiled Viper is, it's in some other time. Sparr came to the wrong time and place. He's stuck here."

Galen frowned. "Except that he's not."

"What do you mean?" asked Keeah.

"Well," said the young wizard, "just before the goblins cornered me, I discovered Salamandra's secret. I know how she has become so powerful and so feared."

"How?" asked Eric.

Galen stepped down the passage to the next tunnel. He looked both ways. "You'll understand better if I show you," he said. "And judging by how long I've been here, it must be nearly dawn. So we need to hurry. Follow me!"

The boy wizard scampered down the passage.

The kids looked at one another.

"I guess we follow him?" said Julie.

"I guess we do!" said Keeah.

A moment later, Eric, Keeah, Neal, Julie, and Max all raced into the passage after the young wizard, Galen Nobeard.

Nine

What's Under the Fortress

The small band wormed its way up through the lower levels of Salamandra's fortress.

At every turn, they heard the echo of goblins howling.

"That noise is driving me nuts," said Neal, holding his stomach. "I think I can understand some of what they're moaning about. And believe me, it's not good."

"Salamandra controls their minds," said Galen, pausing a moment, looking both ways, then heading on again.

"Urik told us a little about Salamandra," said Keeah. "But we didn't have time to hear it all."

"From what my mother could discover in early histories of the world," Galen said, darting up a narrow set of stairs, "there was a city long ago called Pesh. It was one of the earliest cities on Earth, and one of its worst. Its princess was called Salamandra, a young and very wicked sorceress. Stories say she gained power by stealing it from others."

"Not a nice person," said Julie.

"No," said Galen.

"Was she the great-great-grandmother of this one?" asked Julie. "Because this princess looks pretty young."

The boy paused and turned at the top of the stairs. "It's the same person," he said.

"What?" said Eric. "She can't be *that* old. She looks like a teenager."

"She is but a few years older than me," said Galen. "Salamandra devised a way to make the city of Pesh fly through time. It steals magic from wherever it lands, then moves on to the next place and time."

"Fly through time?" said Eric.

Yes! whispered the voice of Sparr in Eric's head. *Through time! Right to where the Coiled Viper is hidden. And you, Eric, will help me. You must!*

Eric's forehead throbbed. *You again? I won't help you!*

But Salamandra . . . is . . . ahhhhh!

The voice faded.

Sparr? said Eric. *What's happening?*

There was no answer.

Max was trembling. "Excuse me, my master-to-be, are you saying that Salamandra has brought Pesh — all of this — out of the *past*?"

Galen nodded slowly. "And if Sparr has become as wicked as you say, then Pesh is the very worst place for him to be. Because from here, he can go anywhere, anytime."

As they ascended through the passages, the walls around them grew hot. The floor thundered suddenly. Then came the sound of loud hammering.

"What's going on?" asked Neal.

"You'll see." Galen led them through one twisting passage after another until they came to an opening onto a narrow ledge. The ledge overlooked a deep pit.

Ssss! Plumes of hot vapor hissed up in clouds from the bottom.

Max waved away the mist and, clutching Neal and Julie, looked over the edge. "Oh, my!"

"Holy cow!" said Eric. "What is that?"

What stood below them was a giant machine.

Blam-chunka-chunka-blam-blam-ssss!

Huge hammers rose and fell with a thundering noise. Giant rods pumped, great open pipes plumed clouds of steam, wheels turned, chains clattered, and gears ground noisily.

"What is it for?" asked Keeah. "What does it do?"

Galen tried to find the right words. "This machine creates a portal, a sort of door through time. Soon it will move Pesh to a new time and place, to steal magic from there, too."

"Holy moly, she's got her own personal time machine!" exclaimed Neal.

"Exactly," said the wizard.

Ssss! Another cloud of steam puffed up and the machine seemed to work a little faster.

"Pesh landed here as an island exactly a year ago," said Galen. "Salamandra sent her goblins out to collect all the magic they could find. Now, after a year of stealing, they have come back. Pesh's next stop — whenever and wherever that is — will suffer even worse."

The kids peered down into the noisy pit.

"So this is why there's almost no magic left in our world," said Julie.

Keeah took a deep breath. "How can we stop such a huge machine?"

Galen grinned at his new friends, laced his fingers together, cracked his knuckles, took a deep breath, and said, "Well, that's just the thing about machines, you know. They break down."

Eric glanced at the young wizard. "Let me guess. You're going to help it along a bit?"

"Just a bit," said Galen. "Now, does anybody want to volunteer to help me shut down this time machine?"

"I will!" Max chirped loudly. "I want to save our friends' wonderful world. And my own. Besides, this is our first adventure together. We must get to know each other."

"Adventure?" said Galen, raising his eyebrows. "You just said the magic word."

"Oh, if only my old master were here to see this!" said Max.

Young Galen smiled. "If what you say is true, then I guess I *was* here to see this. Everyone ready? Then here we gooooooo!"

With a running start, the young wizard and his new spider troll friend leaped together into the grinding, thumping, hissing, thundering pit.

"Good luck!" Keeah called down to them.

An instant later — *ssss!* — a puff of steam rose up, and Galen and Max were lost in the mists of the giant machine.

Julie bit her lip. "I sure hope they make it."

"They better," said Eric. "The future of both worlds depends on them."

"Or on us, if they don't succeed," said Keeah.

Neal raised his hand. "What happens if Galen and Max actually do bust up that hunk of junk? I mean, will Pesh, like, self-destruct?"

Everyone looked at one another.

"Uh-oh," said Eric. "We'd better hurry up and find Sparr."

"But how?" asked Julie. "The place is swarming with goblins. They're not going to let us just march into Salamandra's icky old throne room. Anyone have any ideas?"

Neal made a strange face. "Uh . . . I just have one thing to say . . . *roooorrroww!*"

The others stepped back.

"Neal?" said Keeah.

"Uh, what I actually mean to say is . . . *roooorrroww!*"

Neal blinked, he frowned, he twitched, he shivered, then he began to change.

His face grew long. His skin turned a sickly shade of green. And his nose, the one that was so good at sniffing pies, stretched into a snout — long and bumpy and tipped with whiskers.

With one great final shudder — *ploink!* — Neal had become a goblin.

Ten

A Riddle Among Riddles

Neal looked closely at his green, clawed hands.

"Uh-oh," he said. "This can't be good. It was the pie, wasn't it? It was the pie. Oh, that Jabbo! If I ever get my hands on him again — my weird *green* hands — oh!"

His friends walked completely around him.

"Oww!" he squealed. "Who stepped on

my tail? I mean — yikes! — I have a tail! Oh, this is not good at all!"

Keeah laughed suddenly. "No, it *is* good. In fact, it's perfect!"

"And just how do you figure that?" Neal asked, carefully running his new claws down the length of his new snout.

"Because," she said, "you just found us a way into Salamandra's throne room."

"Oh, no. No way. Keeah, you have to change me back." Then he gasped. "Wait. You *can* change me back, can't you?"

"Of course I can!" she said. "Or Galen can. Or maybe Urik. I think. But anyway, not just yet."

"Keeah's right," said Eric. "Looking the way you do, we'll get into the throne room easily. We can stop Sparr and Salamandra from joining forces. And we can take Sparr back to Droon."

Neal grumbled. "Sure, sure, use the poor kid who turns into the ugly goblin. What I don't do to save the world! All right. Only don't step on my tail. It's sensitive. And actually, so is my hearing. I hear someone coming —"

Fwit-fwit-fwit! Before they could move, a figure flitted down the hall toward them, his face lit with a purple glow. He smiled when he saw them.

"Urik!" said Eric. "You made it. You got free of the kraken!"

The man held up his wand. "Of course. Did you find Galen?"

They told him where his brother was.

"Good," he said. "With a goblin as a cover, I don't think you'll need my help. I'll go find Max and Galen. Funny, that old boatman told me to take good care of Galen. He said his own future depended on it. Strange old man. Anyway, I'd better get going. See you later!"

He raced away as quickly as he had come.

"Okay, then," said Neal. "Let's do this!"

Five minutes later, the four friends were heading down a passage toward the throne room. The hoots and howls from the end of the hall told them that they had come to the right place.

Two goblins guarded a large black door.

Keeah nudged Neal. "We'll keep our hoods low. You tell the guards we want to go in."

Neal sighed and marched up to the guards. "Hey, fellow ugly goblins, I'm looking for Salamandra. You know, about this tall, yellow eyes, bunch of thorns instead of hair?"

The guards eyed him from head to foot.

"What are the magic words?" one asked.

Neal grinned, showing two rows of bumpy teeth. "My mommy taught me those. *Please* and *thank you!*"

"*What* and *what?*" said the second guard, reaching for a sword.

Julie whispered into Neal's large green ear. "How about . . ."

"Oh, yeah!" Neal nodded, coughed, then said, "Would the magic words be . . . Om — yee — Pesh?"

"Oh! At once, sir!" both guards said, bowing low and thrusting the doors open instantly.

"Thank you, my good sirs," said Neal.

"Good and ugly," said Eric under his breath.

The friends entered a giant room.

Wild, thorny plants grew up in every corner and hung down from the walls.

Blazing fiery cauldrons sat on platforms

on each side of the room, casting golden light on hundreds of goblins standing at attention.

"Salamandra!" they chanted. "Salamandra!"

Their chanting echoed around the room and up to an enormous crystal dome at the top. Visible beyond the dome was the brightening sky of morning.

Eric stiffened suddenly as they made their way along the wall. In the center of the room, under a canopy of long, curving thorns, at the top of a set of stairs, was the throne they had seen in the street.

But this time Salamandra wasn't in it.

"Holy cow," Eric whispered.

Sitting on the throne was . . . Lord Sparr.

The sorcerer glared out at the army of goblins, his hands clutching the arms of the throne.

Keeah gasped. "Look at him. He's already made a deal with her. An evil deal, no doubt!"

A trumpet sounded, another set of doors opened on the far side of the room, and all the goblins bowed. "Princess Salamandra!" they bellowed.

Ssss! The flames in the giant pots flared and leaped up when she entered, but the room itself seemed to darken and go ice-cold.

"Is she evil or what?" whispered Julie.

"Evil," said Eric. "Even the fire knows it."

"I'm going to have nightmares about this for a long, long time to come," Neal murmured.

"You have done well, my goblins!" said Salamandra, slowly approaching the throne, holding her thorny staff high. "My treasure rooms are full. My power continues to grow. We've robbed this time of nearly all its magic. The hour has come — it's time to move on."

Deep in her voice was a sound like the howling of dogs or wolves wailing in the night.

"She's just like Sparr," whispered Keeah. "It figures he would join together with her. They're two of a kind."

Eric eyed the sorcerer. *Maybe*, he thought.

But there was something else in Sparr's look as he gazed from the throne. It was almost as if . . .

No, it couldn't be. . . .

Sparr, can you hear me?

Salamandra spoke again. "I have learned the riddles of the ancient rulers of earth and sea. I have stolen the great magics of every age. And yet you, Lord Sparr of Droon, have told me a tale of a Dark Stair and of a great magic that lies hidden in another time. . . ."

Sparr did not rise from the throne. "As we agreed," he said, "I shall use your time portal to find it. And you shall take whatever magic remains —"

Sparr sat up high in Salamandra's throne, and the princess herself circled slowly beneath it, but something was wrong.

Eric could feel it.

Eric . . .

Sparr's voice sounded faintly in his head.

What's going on here? Eric asked.

Salamandra paused, then rose, step-by-step, toward Sparr. Her long cape flowed behind her, its thorns scratching the stairs like fingernails scraping a chalkboard.

"What is the Coiled Viper, Sparr?" she asked.

"All in due time," the sorcerer replied.

The princess stopped. "No," she said. "Now!"

Flang! A thorn shot from her staff and struck the floor at Sparr's feet. In an instant, thorns sprouted from the floor and whipped around him, trapping him in a cage of thorns.

"What?" boomed Sparr, struggling. "You lied to me! You gave your word! You — tricked me!"

The thorns circled up to his shoulders and stopped there, enclosing him on the throne.

"Whoa!" said Neal. "Talk about plans backfiring. She's doing our job for us! This is good."

"Um . . . I don't think it's so good," said Eric.

Salamandra rose to the throne. "Perhaps now you will tell me what I want to know. What is this great magic Viper hidden in this world?"

Sparr said nothing.

Nothing . . . out loud.

His words filled Eric's head.

Eric! hissed the voice of Sparr. *Eric. She is pushing her way into my mind . . . getting nearer to our secret. . . . Her power . . . is strong. . . .*

"You cannot resist me," said the princess.

"Oh, my gosh!" Eric pulled his friends to him. "Salamandra wants what Sparr's looking for. She's sort of breaking into his mind. He's trying not to tell her that he has part of the magic with him. And that . . . I have part of it. I think he's trying to protect me, to protect us."

"Sparr is protecting *us*?" said Keeah. "What do you mean? How do you know?"

Eric breathed in deeply, then thrust his hand into his pocket. The blue gem burned his fingers, but he ignored the pain. He

dragged it out of his pocket and showed the gem to his friends.

Eric's hand trembled as he held the tiny stone. "Sparr gave this to me. It's one of the eyes of the Coiled Viper —"

For the first time since Sparr had given the stone to him, Eric felt like himself again. It was as if the spell were suddenly lifted. Bright blue sparks flickered from his fingertips.

Instantly, Sparr's eyes sought him out. *She is too powerful for me!* he whispered.

Salamandra howled suddenly. "So! Yes! Your mind cannot lie. I do not yet know what this Viper is, but I know *when* it is! Prepare now to witness my power, Lord Sparr of Droon. Goblins of the Time Portal — come! I know where we shall go next!"

The six tall goblins the kids had seen following Salamandra in the street entered the room chanting, "Om — yee — Pesh! Peshhhh!"

A giant flying lizard loped in after them.

It was the same lizard the kids had once seen flying over their town. It had many wings and legs.

As the chanting grew louder, the giant machine in the rooms below grew louder, too.

Blam-chunka-chunka-blam-blam-ssss!

And the crystal dome above them began to open.

"Behold the Portal of Ages!" said Salamandra.

The golden disks hovering above the city shot beams of light from one to the other, forming a giant circle of light overhead.

A sudden rushing wind swept into the room.

"Come, my goblins," Salamandra shouted. "We shall find what Lord Sparr seeks. My empire will rule in every age!"

A storm of air grew above the dome, like the funnel of a tornado, spinning around and around until its hugeness covered the entire city.

The children could feel the floor moving and quivering. The machine was thundering and booming down below.

"Portal, open!" Salamandra commanded.

Everyone, even the goblin army, looked up, transfixed by the sight. It was hazy at first, then gradually became clearer as the funnel of whirling air grew deeper and deeper.

At first, there were the shadows of caves carved into hills, then rough stone buildings.

There were giant pyramids and great

statues, then sailing ships crashing over vast seas, and carriages drawn by horses on country roads. Finally, there were paved streets and tall buildings made of glass.

"It's going into our time!" said Julie, trembling.

"Come on, Galen and Max," Neal whispered. "Come on, Urik. Break that machine. Break it!"

"I see a street," said Julie. "Cars whizzing by."

Sparr was staring at Eric through his cage of thorns. *You know . . . you've always known.*

"No . . . no . . ." Eric whispered.

But he already knew what he would see. He didn't know why or how, but he was sure of it. He stared into the whirling winds. And there it was. A valley surrounded by three hills, covered with fruit trees.

And in the distance he saw a house.

A light brown house with a garage, a driveway, a blue door, and blue shutters.

Eric staggered back. "Oh . . ."

What he saw scared him to death.

What he saw . . . was his own house.

Eleven

Winds of Time

"I know when the Coiled Viper lies hidden!" Salamandra shouted. "And now my prisoner, Sparr, shall help me find it!"

The portal spun around faster and faster, and the city of Pesh rocked below it, as if it would lift right out of the sea and fly up into the swirling funnel. And into the future.

"Salamandra, in our time, in our neighborhood?" said Julie. "We can't let that happen!"

Eric gasped. "But it *did* happen. We saw those goblins come to our street. And that big fat flying lizard, too. They did get there! We saw them! Only now that we're in the past we have a chance to stop them from ever getting there. And the only way to do that is by letting Sparr win. At least this once. Guys, we need to help Sparr."

"Help Sparr?" said Neal. "But he's been our enemy, like, forever —"

"Look," said Eric. "I don't know what this Viper thingy is, but if somebody doesn't stop her, Salamandra will go after it, taking Pesh to our time — to our town! There won't be a lot of magic there, but she won't need it. If she finds the Viper, she'll have even more power. Maybe more than all of us put together."

As the time portal widened, Keeah looked at Eric. "I think you're right."

"Me, too," said Julie. "All of us together, including Sparr, might be able to stop her."

"Hey, I'm just a goblin, and I believe you," said Neal. "But we're way outnumbered here. We need some kind of distraction. To get Sparr free, we need to surprise everyone."

At just that moment — *errrrk!* — a giant cart heaped with purple pies squealed into the room.

Behind it huffed the little dragon, Jabbo. His apron was splattered with fruit smudges, and there were flecks of flour on his bumpy snout.

"Oh, dear," he squealed. "Is Jabbo late again?"

The goblins all turned to the cart, and another rumbling started in the room. The rumbling of stomachs. All the goblins were hungry.

Eric grinned. "We need a surprise, huh? Well, what's more surprising than a pie in the face?"

Neal's green lips edged into a smile. "I like it. But I get to go first!"

"It's a deal," said Eric. "Keeah, you and I have to free Sparr."

She narrowed her eyes. "I'm ready."

While Jabbo was staring up at the spinning portal, and Salamandra was closing in on Sparr once more, Julie and Neal snuck over to the cart and slid several big juicy pies from it.

"Everyone ready?" asked Julie.

They nodded.

In a flash, Julie and Neal leaped to the top of the cart and heaved the pies toward the center of the room. The pies whizzed

through the air. Everyone saw them coming.

Everyone except the evil princess.

Salamandra turned at the last moment
and — *splat-splat-splat-splat!*

Four pies smushed her right in the face.

Salamandra screamed. Jabbo screamed.
The goblins screamed.

"Good shot!" said Julie, high-fiving Neal.

"Not bad yourself!" he said. Then, cup-
ping his green hands to his mouth, he
shouted, "Pie fight!"

Jabbo shrieked. "Not my beautiful
pies —"

But in a flash, pies were flying everywhere.

"Keeah, let's go!" cried Eric.

Two goblins sprang at them, but Eric
leaped over their heads, kicking out with
both feet.

Wump-wump! Both goblins fell flat.

"Hey! I flew just like Urik," Eric shouted. "My powers really are back!"

"And not a minute too soon," said Keeah. "Behind you!"

Three more goblins charged them, but Keeah sent out a spray of blue sparks. The goblins crumpled in a tangled heap on the floor.

Meanwhile, Neal and Julie became a pie-throwing machine. *Splat! Splat! Splat!* Pies soared, flew, dived, and dropped everywhere!

Dodging the flying fruit filling, Eric and Keeah raced to Sparr's cage. With twin bolts of blue lightning, they blasted the thorns — *kkk-blam*!

Sparr sprang from the crumbled cage like a wild animal. "I told you you would help me!"

"Goblins, stop them!" cried Salamandra, wiping purple goop from her purple face.

"No, we're going to stop *you*!" said Eric. "Sparr, Keeah, all of us — together!"

For the first time ever, Sparr stood between Eric and Keeah. Grasping their hands in his own and extending them, Sparr turned to Eric.

"Now you will see our power . . . together!"

Whooooom!

The room exploded in purple light as the blue flashes from Keeah and Eric mixed with Sparr's flaming red lightning bolts.

Ka-whammm! Salamandra was thrown across the room, her magic staff's fiery thorns skittering wildly at the walls.

Sparr laughed as a river of red flame blazed from his fingertips. "Now, give me the gem!"

Eric looked into the sorcerer's eyes. He

stared as deeply as Sparr himself had looked into his in the sewers. He wanted to find what Urik hoped to see. He wanted to see hope.

But he saw only coldness and darkness. He almost regretted helping him, setting him free.

No, thought Eric, grasping the jewel tightly. *If there was any goodness there, it was buried so deep . . . so deep. . . .*

"Forget it, Sparr," he said, backing away. "You can't mutter in my head anymore. Just go! But you won't get the jewel. I'm keeping it."

Sparr sneered. "You're no longer under my spell?"

"The minute I told my friends, it was broken."

"Friends, Sparr," said Keeah. "Something you don't have and probably never will."

Sparr glared at the two young wizards. "We shall meet again. And when we do, I shall be more powerful than you can possibly imagine!"

"We'll be waiting," Eric murmured.

"Together," said Keeah.

With a strange look on his face, Sparr smiled. *Our day is coming, Eric Hinkle!*

With that, Sparr whirled his cape around him and flew straight up into the whirling funnel.

"Noooo!" cried Salamandra. "That boy, that girl, they did this! It's their fault. I'll get you —"

Suddenly — *rrrrrr!* The portal quivered and wobbled. The whirling tunnel of air began to collapse at the far end.

Salamandra fell to her knees, howling.

At that instant, young Galen burst in, with Max skittering behind.

"We wrecked the Portal of Ages," Galen

yelped. "Pesh is going back to where it came from. The ancient past!"

"And we don't have much time left!" said Max.

"No pies, either," said Julie. "We're out."

"Then it's a good thing I'm here!" said a voice.

And there was Urik, leaping in, his purple wand flashing into the crowd of goblins, sending them reeling back to their princess in a squirming heap of green and purple.

"Where's Sparr?" asked Galen. "Was he here?"

Eric pointed up to the wobbling portal. "He's gone . . . into the future."

"But thanks to you," said Keeah, "the portal will collapse before he gets too far. He'll be lost in time."

"Then I'm going after him," said Urik,

handing his satchel to his younger brother. "If there's an ounce of our mother's goodness in him, I'll find it. Take the wand, Galen. It's yours now. Do good things with it."

"But, Urik —" Galen started to say.

It was too late. Urik leaped into the whirling light as Sparr had done. A moment later, he was gone.

"I — will — destroy — you!" Salamandra cried, turning her magic staff on the children.

Thwing! Thwing! Sharp flaming thorns flew like bullets at them.

Eric leaped up and dodged the thorns, but when he came back down — *clack!* — the tiny blue gem fell out of his hand and spun across the floor toward her, glowing as if it were alive.

"No," he said. "She can't get it —"

"Eric, here!" called Galen. He tossed Urik's wand.

Salamandra rushed for the gem, but Eric caught the wand and turned it on her.

Kkkkk! With its last gasp of power, the wand shot out a bright purple bolt of light.

Salamandra collapsed to the floor, crying in defeat. But just as she fell, so did the final petal of the wand.

Eric watched, stunned, as the petal vanished and the purple light faded from the air.

Instantly, the Wand of Urik twisted and bent in his hand. And it became no more than a rough and crooked stick.

Salamandra rose to her feet at last. "Goblins, if I can't have this world, at least I'll have Droon!"

In a flash, she was gone from the throne room.

The fortress wobbled and quivered suddenly, sending the gem sliding into the shadows.

Shrieking, the goblins raced after the princess, while Jabbo yelped and hid under his pie cart.

"The gem," said Eric. "I have to get it. . . ."

The floor quaked and heaved.

"Leave it," said Julie. "It's better off buried in the past. But we shouldn't be — come on!"

"Pesh is going back in time!" cried Max.

"Let's get out of here," said Keeah. "Back to the Dark Stair."

"Yeah," said Neal. "While we still have a chance!"

Twelve

New Friends, New Foes

Splash! Sploosh! Vrrrm!

By the time the kids reached the water, Salamandra's sleek green boat was speeding away.

"She'll find Droon," said Max. "She'll try to destroy it, too."

Keeah looked across the canals to see the sunlight glinting off the jeweled door on the far shore. "We'll never stop her in time."

"Ho, there! Do you need a ride?" called a voice. The old boatman waved from the water, his beat-up canal boat bobbing on the waves.

"Excuse me, but in that old boat?" said Neal. "We need something a little faster —"

"Ah, but while you were inside, I've been making improvements," the boatman said with a chuckle. "Hurry. The goblin boats are coming."

Eeeee! Rrrr! The kids turned to see a dozen black boats roar out of the tunnels under the fortress. Each boat had sharp green fins sticking up from the back.

"After them!" the goblins howled.

"I guess we have no choice," said Keeah, jumping into the old boat. "Let's ride!"

Julie, Eric, Neal, Max, and the young Galen joined her. Everyone held on as the boat roared over the water, seeming to fly above the waves.

"There's some spell at work here," said young Galen, beginning to grin. "It's very much like something I would do —"

"It's *exactly* like something you would do," said the old boatman. "Or should I say — like *we* would do?"

He tossed off his floppy hat. His white hair blew in the wind. His long beard whipped over his shoulder.

"Galen?" cried Keeah. "It's you!"

The old wizard bowed. "It's me!"

"And — me!" said young Galen. He rubbed his eyes and laughed. "Well! It's good to know I'm still here after five hundred years!"

Old Galen sped the boat into a narrow channel, with two goblin boats roaring in after them. "I'm sorry I could not join you in the fortress. You had your own trials to face in there. Excuse me —"

He jerked the rudder to the left and flitted into a side passage. Racing to the end, he sent up a huge spray of water.

Fwooosh! The two goblin pilots were washed overboard, leaving their empty boats blocking the way. *Wham-wham-wham!* Three more boats crashed into them.

"Goblin pileup!" said Eric.

"Serves them right!" said Julie.

Galen's younger self laughed, together with the old wizard. "I see you still like to live dangerously!"

"I do!" said the bearded old man. "And speaking of danger, I see our old friend is back. Kraken off the port side!"

Roooaooooow! The kraken splashed out of the water and leaped for the boat, spitting black water all over the place.

"That does it!" growled Neal. "I've really had it with this guy! Kraken, it's payback time!"

Neal thrust his goblin face right at the sea monster and roared at the top of his lungs.

Roooaoooow!

The kraken's big eyes bulged with fear. Then Neal swatted its snout, and the sea monster silently sank back into the water.

"Ha-ha!" Julie crowed. "You did it! That's two *more* points for the ugly goblin!"

"And now," said Eric. "To the Dark Stair!"

Galen piloted the boat swiftly and carefully to the far shore, landing at the docks near the Dirty Plate.

"Come on, everyone!" cried Keeah, leaping from the boat. She led the small band through the quaking streets to the foot of the Dark Stair.

Even as they got there, the evil princess Salamandra was racing up the black steps to the jeweled door.

At the top, she turned.

Thwing! Thwing! She shot one flaming thorn after another at the kids. Keeah and the two Galens made a shield of blue light.

Plink! Plank! The thorns fell away harmlessly.

Salamandra glared at them. "Fancy work, wizards. But you haven't seen the last of me!"

"That's what they all say," Eric called back.

With a sneer, the sorceress slipped through the jeweled door and down the far side into Droon.

"We'll get you!" cried Max, scampering up the stairs. "Evil princess!"

"I fear we shall find her soon enough,

my friend," said the old wizard as the city quivered and grew suddenly hazy.

"Pesh will soon return to its distant past," said old Galen. "One thing only remains to be done here." He turned to his younger self. "You must stay in this world. You have a great task to accomplish. You must create the rainbow stairs."

Young Galen looked at his older self. "Is that how I get to Droon?"

"It is. And your journey begins now."

The boy smiled. "A journey? Is there danger?"

The old wizard laughed. "Plenty of that, and mystery, too! Oh, the things I could tell you —"

"Master!" said Max, giving old Galen a look.

"Hmm? Yes, quite right, Max, quite right. You must experience it all yourself.

But know this, young self. With friends, all things are possible."

The boy wizard smiled and looked at Eric, Keeah, Julie, Neal, and especially Max. "I think I just found that out. Well, then, point me in the right direction. Where will I create these stairs?"

"I think I know!" said Julie. She took Urik's map from the brown satchel and opened it. "First, you have to cross this wide ocean."

"Then look for a valley in the middle of three hills," said Eric. "There you'll find the perfect spot to create the rainbow stairs. Someday, a house will be built over it. My house."

"That's what starts the whole great adventure," said Keeah.

"And now for the wand," said the old man.

Eric took it from his belt. "But it's all used up. It's just a plain stick now."

Old Galen looked at it. "When you found it, it was a stick, yet it became a wand. Now, see what happens."

The young wizard took the stick in his hand. Suddenly, it straightened and turned blue, then red, then gold. Finally, a purple flower full of petals blossomed from the end and began to glow.

"Cool!" said Eric. "I guess it's your turn now."

The boy smiled. "A map, the wand. All I need now is a sailing ship."

"And it waits for you." The old wizard pointed to the shore where their small boat bobbed at the docks. All of a sudden, the frail craft stretched in every direction, masts grew from a wide deck, and shimmering sails unfurled.

It sat atop the water, a glinting, silvery craft.

"That's a boat fit for an adventure!" said Max.

"Now *there's* a magic word if I ever heard one!" said old Galen. "Go. Create the stairs!"

"I will," said the boy. He raced to the shore and hopped aboard the boat. Instantly, wind filled its sails, and it rolled away from Pesh.

"But master," said Max. "Do we ever see your brother Urik again?"

The wizard sighed. "Ah. His tale is an interesting one. And I suspect you will also want to hear about Sparr, too, and why I never told you who he was. That, my dear friends, is a long story. But it's one that I shall tell you — what? Oh!"

A sudden flash of brown hurtled past

Galen, up the stairs, and right through the jeweled door.

Keeah gasped. "What was that?"

Neal sniffed. "Uh-oh. I think it's . . . Hey, if I'm right, we'd better hurry!"

Everyone scrambled up the stairs and leaped through the door just as Pesh quaked for the last time and faded completely into the mist.

"I was right." Neal pointed down the stairs.

There was something sprinkled on the shiny black steps to Droon. A fine white powder.

"Flour?" asked Julie. "You mean, that was — Jabbo? Jabbo's gone to Droon, too?"

"Oh, yeah!" squeaked a high voice. "And he's gonna rule the whole place!"

There, below them, darting down into the pink sky of Droon, was the little dragon, Jabbo.

In his hand was a tiny blue gem. When its glow shone on his bumpy snout, he puffed out a great roar of flame and shouted, "Jabbo's got the power now. Jabbo will rule Droon!"

Max groaned. "Oh, no. Here we go again!"

Quickly, Keeah and Galen closed the jeweled door, chanting words of ancient Droon over and over until the door seemed to fade away, just as Pesh itself had done.

"That should keep it closed," said Keeah. "Besides, you can't open what you can't find."

They raced down the Dark Stair and into the land of Droon once more. At the bottom stood the great white summit of Silversnow, just as they had left it. Salamandra and Jabbo were nowhere in sight.

"I'll search for footprints," said Max.

Off he scurried, with his nose to the ground.

Eric shot a look at Keeah. She was gazing up at the top of the Dark Stair, even as her face was lit by the sun rising over her own world.

"Are you thinking what I'm thinking?" he asked. "I mean, that was one strange adventure."

Keeah nodded. "I understand more clearly than ever that our worlds are bound together. The future of one with the past of the other."

"And the other way around, too," said Neal.

Julie sighed. "It's sort of sad that there's so little magic left in our world. It explains a lot."

Keeah smiled. "Galen said that there was *some* left. I think he means all of you."

At that moment, there came a soft whooshing sound behind them. Turning, they saw the shimmering rainbow stairs.

The stairs that young Galen had created.

Keeah turned to the old wizard. "So you did find the way to the New World. You used your brother's wand. You made the stairs."

"I did indeed," Galen said. "And all is as it should be."

"Ahem!" said Neal, raising a green claw. "All is as it should be? I mean, hello? Goblin here!"

Julie laughed. "And we were just getting used to you, too. You were handy to have around."

"Hold still," said Galen. "Now let me see. Ah, yes. Erom — on — nilbog!"

Ploink! Neal's snout shrank away, his

feet returned to normal, and his skin's deep green color faded. He was just plain Neal again.

"I have to say," Keeah said with a smile, "you really were kind of cute."

Neal blinked. "Now you tell me!"

Max scampered over. "Look, everyone! Our two new enemies went different ways!"

He pointed to two sets of footprints, one streaked with thorn marks, the other made by the wide, clawed feet of a dragon.

"Yes, yes," said Galen, wrapping his long blue cloak around him. "I'm afraid we have a sorceress and a dragon loose in Droon. Duty calls us. Max, Keeah, let's be off!"

Keeah turned to her friends and shrugged. "There's never a dull moment! Until next time!"

Waving, she and Max ran off after Galen.

"I guess it's our turn, too," said Neal.

As their Droon friends set off on their new adventure, Eric, Neal, and Julie raced across the snowy summit to the glittering rainbow stairs.

They charged up the steps, then Julie stopped.

"What is it?" asked Neal.

"Do you think . . . I mean, will we ever see Sparr again?" she asked. "After all, he's sort of lost in time somewhere."

Eric remembered Sparr's last words to him.

Our day is coming. . . .

"I guess . . . only time will tell," he said.

"Speaking of time," said Neal. "It must be snack time. My stomach's grumbling. I feel like pie."

Julie laughed. "Neal, haven't you learned your lesson about pie?"

"I'll take my chances," said Neal. "Let's go!"

Glancing once more at the magical world of Droon, Eric, Neal, and Julie turned and raced up the rainbow stairs for home.

ABOUT THE AUTHOR

Tony Abbott is the author of more than forty funny novels for young readers, including the popular *Danger Guys* books and *The Weird Zone* series. Since childhood he has been drawn to stories that challenge the imagination, and, like Eric, Julie, and Neal, he often dreamed of finding doors that open to other worlds. Now that he is older — though not quite as old as Galen Longbeard — he believes he may have found some of those doors. They are called books. Tony Abbott was born in Ohio and now lives with his wife and two daughters in Connecticut.

For more information about Tony Abbott and the continuing saga of Droon, visit *www.tonyabbottbooks.com*.